Disaster in

Aloha

By

Helen Kaulbach

DISASTER IN ALOHA

Copyright © 2016 Helen Kaulbach

ISBN 978-1539771616

Electronic Version published - Amazon Kindle
Print Version published: Creatspace

Author: Helen Kaulbach
E-mail: kaulbach45@gmail.com

Dedicated to Dougie, the love of my life and my favorite travelling companion, who loves visiting Hawaii as much as I do.

Many thanks to my daughter, Kristal Kaulbach, and her colleague, Julie Backer, for their proofreading and editing expertise and help with some technical details.

Cover photography and design by Helen Kaulbach.
Thanks to Gabriele Raasch for technical help with cover.

Table of Contents

Chapter 1

Chapter 2

Chapter 3

Chapter 1

The weather office at Honolulu International Airport was busy. Sundays usually were.

There were more flights going back to the mainland on Sunday than any other day. Vacationers, here for a week or two, always chose to stay until Sunday, even if it meant arriving back at work on Monday morning red-eyed from lack of sleep and fuzzy-headed from jet lag.

Jamie Pitt, first officer with Aloha Pacific Air, stood just inside the door enjoying the air conditioning. He was just coming off a three-day layover in Honolulu, had been surfing earlier that morning, and was still on the beach at 10 a.m., leaving himself barely an hour to shower and change before he had to be at the airport. Single and just 30, he loved the Hawaiian lifestyle and took as much downtime in Hawaii as he could get.

Captain Dick Reynolds, 50ish and distinguished looking with a touch of gray in his hair, was already at the desk checking the satellite weather map. He looked up as Jaime leaned over the map.

"That a blank map you got there, Cap'n? Or is the weather really that good?" joked Jamie

"Clear as a bell all the way to LAX"

"Sounds like a boring trip."

"Best kind," said Reynolds, a 24-year veteran with Aloha Pacific. "I'll take boring any day over excitement when I'm in the cockpit."

"You're losing your edge, old man. You can nap today and I'll take us home."

"As soon as we're airborne I might take you up on that."

A couple of miles away, across Honolulu Bay, the famous Aloha Tower glistened in the sunshine. Built in the 1930's to welcome cruise ships, it was still a fixture on the Honolulu waterfront and a draw to tourists. The elevator to the observation deck at the top disgorged its load of sightseers and filled up again.

A couple, obviously tourists, who were walking through the shopping plaza at the base of the tower, stopped to gaze up at the people on the observation deck.

"Oh, Bubba, the view from up there must be fantastic. Let's go up!"

Bubba lifted his baseball cap for a better view of the edifice, hitched up his pants which were buckled precariously low under an enormous belly, and started walking again. "Let's eat first before the lunch crowds get here. Maybe after lunch the line-up will be shorter."

Mimi, Bubba's wife, a skinny little thing half his size with a long-suffering look on her face, followed behind him. When Bubba's mind was on food nothing distracted him. Not that he really needed it. The brightly flowered Hawaiian shirt he'd bought when they arrived a week ago was already straining the buttons.

A cab pulled up to the Pacific Air entrance to the terminal. A sunburned redhead flounced out of the back seat, slamming the door before the other occupant could follow. She stalked into the terminal and headed for the restroom leaving her new husband to pay the driver and cope with their luggage on his own.

Jeremy Stevenson climbed slowly out of the cab and went to the back of the vehicle to collect their bags. The driver pressed the catch and tried to open the trunk. It wouldn't budge. He pounded his fist on it a couple of times and bounced the back of the cab up and down. The trunk stayed closed. Jeremy added his strength to the driver's. The trunk still stayed closed.

The driver shrugged his shoulders. "Man, I gotta take this cab back to the garage to get this open."

"You're not going anywhere with my luggage inside. I've got a flight to catch and I'm not leaving without my luggage." Jeremy, already red in the face from the sun and the recent fight with his wife, got redder still. "You better find someone right now to open that trunk or I'll rip it apart with a crowbar." He beckoned to a security guard by the terminal door, and explained the problem. The security guard, a big, burly fellow, had a go at opening the cab trunk. It wouldn't budge.

By this time five minutes had passed and a crowd had gathered, laughing and making suggestions.

Jeremy looked over the rag-tag group gathered around the cab and muttered, "Where is a good crook when I need one? Last week on Sunset Beach someone broke into my rental car in less than 30 seconds."

Amid all the laughter and back-slapping from the group, one man stepped forward with a screwdriver in his hand. He felt along the edge of the trunk, located what he was looking for, stuck the screwdriver in and gave it a twist. The trunk popped open. Giving Jeremy a grin, he melted back into the crowd, leaving the cab driver open-mouthed in protest.

"Damn! He ruined the lock on my trunk. Who's gonna pay for fixing it?"

Jeremy lifted the two large bags out of the trunk, hung his carry-on bag around his neck and started into the terminal, calling over his shoulder, "That's your problem, Mac. I'm outta here."

He staggered through the sliding doors with his load, his temper still high. Not sure, at this point, if he was angrier at Jacquie for the argument they had in the cab or for leaving him with all the luggage. His anger at the cab driver had diminished and he was starting to see the funny side of it, already going over in his mind how he would tell the story to his softball buddies back home.

Jacquie, who had the tickets, had already checked in and gotten their boarding passes. She was waiting for him to bring their bags to the check-in. When he'd deposited their bags and received a claim check, Jacquie shoved his ticket and boarding pass at him.

"Here's your seat number for the back of the plane. They had one up-grade to First Class left and I got it. See you back in L.A." Then she turned on her heel and stalked off into the crowd, leaving Jeremy standing there staring after his wife of two weeks.

"Some honeymoon," he muttered, and started walking in the opposite direction. He spotted a bar just outside the security gate. It was going to be a long flight home.

A black family, father, mother and son in his early teens, strode into the courtyard at the base of Aloha Tower. By the way they walked, it was easy to tell that all three were athletes. The teen hung back, checking out some Harley-Davidson T-shirts in one of the kiosks around the courtyard, while his parents continued on to the Tower.

"Come on, C.J.," called the mother, "don't get lost."

C.J. ducked in behind the kiosk, hoping no one would think she was talking to him. *Why did his mother still treat him like a baby? There was no way he could get lost. He knew where they were going.*

"C.J.," yelled his mother from across the courtyard. "Hurry up. Your father's already in the lineup for the elevator."

C.J. hunched his shoulders in embarrassment, as only a 13-year-old can, and slowly made his way across to where his mother was standing. He knew she would keep at him until he caught up with them. This whole family vacation thing wasn't his idea. He would rather be back home riding his bike with his friends and playing ball. Heck, he was even missing an important baseball tournament. His team needed him and he should be there. But no, his PUs, his Parental Units as he referred to them, had decided that they should see more of the country than Mississippi. That since his Dad was a history teacher, they should learn more about the history of their country than just the south. His Mom had wanted to go to New York, but his Dad, for some reason, hated New York. Most of the north too, to hear him talk about it. So Hawaii it was. And now he was stuck here, following his parents around like a little kid, while they were sightseeing. His father wanted to visit every 'historically significant' site on the Islands, but they all looked like plain old tourist traps to him.

Knisha looked at her son sympathetically. She knew he wasn't happy about this trip, that baseball was more important to him than sightseeing. She put her arm around his shoulder and gave him a quick squeeze before he ducked away from her.

"Only three more days," she said to him, smiling. "Then we're heading home and you can play ball the rest of the summer."

They went inside where her husband, Cato, was waving to catch her attention, having already secured their place in the lineup.

Chief Flight Attendant Shari-Lynn Cobbs hurried down the jetway pulling her small bag on its wheels and carrying a briefcase. She stowed them, along with her jacket, in a compartment in the first class section. She was thinking of her two kids. She was glad she'd been able to get weekend flights this month, so Bobby would be home to look after them. Most of the younger girls hated weekend flights because they cut into their social life. But she preferred them. That way, her boys always had one parent at home. She'd be glad to get home tonight. The weather was looking good, so there should be no delays.

"Hi, Mit-su," she called to the diminutive Japanese-American who'd followed her on board. "Glad to see you're working the flight today. How was your weekend?"

"Oooh! Those Hawaiian boys are something else. My grandmother would be rolling in her grave if she could hear some of the things they say to me. But I love it." She giggled as she disappeared into the first class galley. Shari-Lynn laughed too, as she opened her briefcase and started on her pre-flight paperwork. She stopped momentarily to say hello to the pilot and co-pilot as they came on board, and noted the other flight attendants as they started preparing the cabin. By the time the first passengers started filing in she had stowed her briefcase and was smiling as she greeted them.

      Knisha and C.J. squeezed past a young couple with a tiny baby in a stroller to get to where Cato stood. She spoke to him in a low voice for a moment, then satisfied that he wasn't going to start yelling at C.J., she started looking around. The inside of the building was rather plain and not very interesting, so she turned her attention to the people coming in. There was at least one elevator load of people ahead of them and more still coming in. Knisha enjoyed people watching and there were certainly enough different people here to keep her interested, She watched as an elderly Chinese couple joined the line, accompanied by a beautiful young girl about C.J.'s age. Probably their granddaughter. It was getting noisier by the minute, but her head jerked up as a bellow in a southern accent cut through the din.

      "Gol durn it, Mimi, y'all thought the lineup would be shorter after lunch."

      Mimi rolled her eyes skyward. "No, Bubba, it was you who thought that. But we're here now, so let's get in line."

      There was a small break in the line where some people were talking and hadn't moved along right away. Bubba strode purposefully to the break and filled it, whistling and staring straight ahead as if he'd been there all along. The couple whose place he'd taken looked at him and frowned. The man started to say something, then grinned at his wife.

"I'm on vacation so I'm supposed to chill out and stay mellow, eh Mari?" Marianne grinned back at her husband, amused at his attempt to copy the speech patterns of their two teenagers.

"Right on. One space back in the line won't set us back much.....oops, make that two spaces back." Her voice dropped as Mimi sidled up and stood in line next to her husband.

The Chicago newlyweds, Jeremy and Jacquie, were almost the last to board the plane. Jacquie was beginning to regret the snit she'd been in this morning and was planning to apologize before the flight, so she waited for him. When he came out of the bar and she saw he'd been drinking, all thoughts of apologizing flew out of her head. She started to berate him as they walked down the jetway and advised him not to have anything more to drink if he didn't want to embarrass himself.

"Can it, Jacquie," he said as he started toward the back of the aircraft. "We'll talk when we get back home. You're in such a miserable mood this morning, you must have PMS or something."

Jacquie stalked into first class, tossing her red hair and found her seat in the last row of the section. PMS indeed! She never suffered from Pre-Menstrual Syndrome. She didn't even have her period. As she sat there fuming, a man in an airline employee's uniform sat next to her, taking the last seat in first class. Mit-su, the flight attendant, spoke to him, calling him by name as she did her seat belt check. They spoke for a moment before she resumed her check.

As the aircraft taxied out to the runway, Jacquie thought about Jeremy's last remark and started calculating dates. Suddenly she sat bolt upright. If her dates were correct she was about 7 days late. Could she be….was it possible? Maybe there was a reason for her crabbiness the past couple of days. A grin spread across her face. Could she really have gotten pregnant on her honeymoon? How old-fashioned. How delightful. She undid her seatbelt and started to get up. She had to talk to Jeremy right away.

The man sitting next to her grabbed her arm and pulled her back in her seat. She sat there astonished as he reached across and rebuckled her seatbelt.

"Sorry, Miss. The seatbelt sign is on and we're ready for takeoff. You can't go anywhere now."

"But… but, I have to see my husband now. You see, I have something important to tell him."

"It'll have to keep for a few minutes. We'll be airborne in less than a minute and at cruising altitude in about five minutes. You can go to him then." He grinned at her. "Trust me. I'm a pilot. This is no time to go walking the aisles."

Jacquie looked out the window and became aware of the plane gathering speed as it sped down the runway. She settled impatiently back in her seat and closed her eyes. As soon as the seatbelt sign was off, she'd go back and talk to Jeremy.

The elevator in the Aloha Tower disgorged its load of passengers and started to fill again. As they filed in, a lighted sign flashed above the doors, "Capacity 12 persons." Cato, Knisha and C.J. were first, followed by the couple with the baby stroller. They tucked the stroller protectively into a corner and stood close to it. The Chinese couple and their granddaughter were next, followed by Bubba and Mimi. The couple who'd left the teenagers at home, Dave and Marianne from Vancouver, Canada, were last.

The doors were about to close when Bubba stuck out his arm and stopped them. Holding the door open and glowering at the rest of the occupants he protested loudly, "There's 13 people in this elevator!"

Cato frowned disdainfully. "One of them's an infant, for God's sake. My camera equipment weighs more than he does."

"I don't care about weight," Bubba said, "I'm not riding in no elevator with 13 people. Unlucky is what it is." He looked around at the others. Nobody moved. Then he pointed to the next person waiting in line, a Hawaiian girl in her teens, standing alone and carrying a lunch bag.

"You!" he bellowed.

The girl jumped and pointed to herself. "Me?" she squeaked.

"Yes, you. You're small and we already have a couple of kids in here. One more won't matter. I ain't going up in no elevator with 13 on board." He beckoned and she stepped into the elevator.

The doors slid closed.

Captain Dick Reynolds sat seemingly relaxed in the left-hand cockpit seat.

The relaxed demeanor was an act born of long experience. In reality he was alert, every sense attuned to the sounds and feel of his aircraft. Their A340-600 Airbus, built for long-haul flights over water, was his favorite aircraft. It was a sweet one to fly and after three years he knew it well – all its creaks, groans and oil leaks.

Was it his imagination, or did he just feel a slight shudder in the left rudder. His eyes roamed over the dials and instruments in front of him. Nothing was any different than when he'd checked them two minutes ago. He glanced over at his First Officer, Jamie Pitt. Jamie was almost finished his pre-flight checklist and he, too, looked relaxed. So far, he hadn't found anything to worry him.

"We're up next," said Jamie quietly. "Checklist is A-OK." When the Captain didn't answer him right away, he looked at him sharply. "Any problem?"

"No, I don't see any problem. But I just thought I felt a bump."

"Probably ran over a pebble on the runway," joked Jeremy.

"Probably. But all the same, I'm going to ease 'er off for a bit and run 'er up again."

They were now poised at the end of the runway, cleared by the tower for takeoff. Reynolds held them there for a few seconds while he eased off the throttles and then ran it up to full power again. Both men scanned the dials again. Nothing was amiss.

Reynolds eased off the brakes and settled firmer into his seat. "Here we go."

The big plane gathered speed quickly and sped down the runway. Halfway along, the nose wheel still hadn't lifted.

Jamie frowned. "We must have a heavy load today."

Reynolds grunted and reached for the throttles, about to abort the takeoff. They were on the 12,000 foot Reef Runway and fast approaching the end when the nose came up and the aircraft leaped into the air. He watched as the end of the runway disappeared underneath. They crossed the narrow channel and flew low over Sand Island and then were out over Honolulu Bay. The noise abatement rule was to bank sharply to the right one kilometer from the end of the runway. They were supposed to fly over the bay, then parallel to Waikiki Beach and Diamond Head before picking up a heading NE to Los Angeles.

He checked the instruments for the correct heading before turning and noticed with alarm that they didn't have enough altitude to bank the aircraft.

A glance out the cockpit told him they were just barely above the waves.

"What the hell...!" he muttered.

Just as Jamie yelled, "What's going on? We're not getting altitude."

The plane climbed a few feet then settled back again. Jamie, who still had an open connection to the tower, yelled, "Mayday! We have a problem."

With the end of the bay looming closer, Reynolds tried frantically to turn the nose of the plane towards open water, away from the downtown area.

Nothing happened. The rudder was useless.

So he did the only thing possible; he cut power to the engines.

The aircraft, with its nose still high, hit the water with a huge splash, then rose into the air again. It rose and fell, skipping across the bay like a pebble skipped on the surface of a smooth lake.

The two pilots watched in horror as the Aloha Tower loomed ever closer.

About 200 yards out, the aircraft settled into the water and they had fleeting hopes that it would slow down and stop in shallow water. But they forgot that the nose wheel was still down. When the wheel hit the shelving bottom of the bay, it was still turning. The momentum carried the plane up the seabed and buried its nose in Aloha Tower about 30 feet above the base. The tail slowly sank underwater.

The last thing Captain Dick Reynolds heard was First Office Jamie Pitt's anguished cry, "Oh shit!"

Chapter 2

Elly ducked her head in embarrassment as she stepped into the elevator. A shy girl who had a summer job as busgirl in a restaurant in the Aloha Shopping Center, she hated being the center of attention. She would have been perfectly happy waiting for the next elevator, but when that awful man called her to get in she went rather than cause a fuss.

As soon as the doors closed, Bubba reached over and hit the "up" button.

The elevator had just started to rise when there was a terrific bang. The whole building shook.

The intake of breath in the tiny space was audible.

The elevator rose sharply, throwing all the occupants off balance, then dipped down at one corner, causing a pile-up in that corner. The baby stroller started to roll. The young mother screamed and grabbed it, then was thrown off balance herself as the elevator righted itself and abruptly dropped about six inches.

There were a series of thuds on the roof of the elevator.

Then the lights went out.

There was silence for about two seconds and then a high-pitched wailing started. It was the elderly Chinese lady who was sitting on the floor, her husband kneeling beside her patting her on the hand and rubbing her shoulder

That was when the others realized they could actually see them and they did have light, dim though it was. When the lights went out, a battery-operated emergency light, up near the ceiling in one corner, came on. There were two small spotlight bulbs, poorly aimed. One was pointed at the wall and only a few inches away so very little light actually entered the room, the other shone straight down into the corner where the hapless Mrs. Chen still wailed, her voice rising and falling in a chant.

"Can't someone shut her up?" growled Bubba, as he struggled to get back on his feet after falling against his wife and squeezing her against the control panel.

The Chens' granddaughter bent down to talk to her grandfather, who in turn spoke soothingly to his wife. Her chanting slowed to a whisper and finally stopped. The granddaughter explained in a low voice that her grandmother wasn't used to elevators and thought they were all going to die. She was singing a traditional Chinese song for the dead.

The noise level in the elevator rose as everyone else got to their feet or pushed away from walls they'd crashed into, rubbing sore shoulders or twisted ankles.

"What the hell's going on?" bellowed Bubba, as he frantically punched all the buttons on the console. "Why doesn't someone open the damn doors and let us out?"

Cato, who was nursing a bruised elbow where he'd slammed into the wall, said testily, "There are women and children in here. Can't you watch your language?"

"I don't give a God damn what you want, boy. I just want out of here."

Cato stiffened at the term "boy" and was about to confront Bubba with his fists raised when Knisha caught his arm and pulled him back.

"He's not worth it, dear. Leave him alone," she whispered.

Dave, the second-last person to get on the elevator, was leaning against the wall staring at his cell phone.

"Does anyone else have a phone? I've got no signal on mine, but as it's a Canadian server it sometimes doesn't work outside the country." Cato pulled out his phone, as did the father of the baby and the young Chinese girl. All three phones showed a no signal screen.

"Aloha Tower is a very old building, built in the 1930's," said Cato. "With the concrete walls, probably a concrete elevator shaft and the steel elevator inside that, this is most likely a cell phone dead zone."

Dave raised his voice to be heard above the groans following that statement.

"I'm a mechanical engineer and I know a little about elevators. This is no ordinary elevator failure. Something else has happened; some outside force. It might be an earthquake, or possibly a semi lost its brakes and crashed into the building. It might even be a terrorist bombing. Whatever it is, we're not the priority. If we were, someone would be forcing those doors right now. I thought I heard sirens a minute ago, but couldn't be sure. Can we all just be quiet for a minute?"

In the silence that followed, they heard sirens and possibly faint screams. There was even a metallic banging somewhere overhead. But nothing sounded close. The elevator shaft and steel elevator with its double doors were effective soundproofing.

Jim, the father of the young baby, spoke up. "I'm an Air Force Sergeant, stationed at

Wright Field here in Honolulu. I'm not privy to top military dispatches, but I do know that the threat of terrorist attacks here on Hawaii is very real. As Aloha Tower is one of our most recognizable landmarks, it would definitely be on the list of targets. So this gentleman here," he nodded towards Dave, "could very well be right. If he is, there are a lot of injured people out there. Looking after them is a priority right now. They'll get to us later."

"Having said that," Cato added, "it might be wise to let someone know we're in here. Perhaps those of us who have loud voices could take turns yelling 'Help' and pounding on the door. How about you, sir," he pointed at Bubba. "Perhaps you would go first."

Bubba jerked upright, unsure whether to be insulted because a black man pointed at him and suggested he do something, or to preen because he had been chosen for an important role. His mind was made up when Mimi punched him in the side.

"Go ahead, Bubba. If anyone can attract attention, you can. Why, they'd prob'ly hear you clear up the Diamond Head."

So Bubba stood in the middle of the floor, took a deep breath and yelled "HELP" several times at the top of his lungs. The sound reverberated around the tiny room causing Marianne to put her hands over her ears. C.J.

and the Chens' granddaughter, Suzi, who up until now had never even acknowledged the other, looked at each other and laughed.

Kathy, the Air Force sergeant's wife grabbed up her baby, but it was too late. The child woke with a start and began to cry.

Cato, meanwhile, was pounding on the door with his fists.

There was no answering sound from outside. Everyone listened hard, but all they could hear was the faint sound of sirens.

Marianne was searching through her purse, but couldn't find what she was looking for. "Does anyone have anything metallic?" she asked. "The sound of metal on metal carries further than dull thuds like fists."

Everyone looked through handbags and pockets, but no one could come up with anything metal larger than a key. Then Dave pointed to the baby stroller.

"Does that come apart?" he asked Jim. "Is there any way we can use a piece of your baby carriage?" Kathy put her hand on it reflexively. Surely they weren't going to take apart her baby stroller. But Jim was already down on his knees examining it.

"It folds, but doesn't come apart easily. However, there's one pipe here under the footrest that would come out if I had a screwdriver."

"Yeah," muttered Cato, under his breath. "Just what I always carry with me....a screwdriver."

"Hey," said Bubba. "No problem." He pulled a large key chain from his pocket and picked out one of the many items dangling from it, a curiously twisted piece of metal. "This here handy-dandy little thingamabob is a combination beer bottle opener, fish scaler and screwdriver. Never leave home without it!" He carefully detached it from the ring and, with a flourish, passed it to Jim.

In less than a minute, Jim had the piece of pipe free and was pounding on the metal elevator door. Everyone was quiet except for the baby who was screaming at the top of his lungs. An embarrassed Kathy started rummaging through the diaper bag hanging on the stroller, found a bottle of milk, uncapped it and put the nipple in the child's mouth, The cries stopped immediately and satisfied sucking sounds could be heard.

Everyone listened again, but there was still no answering knock. There were groans of discouragement and everyone started talking again.

Everyone, that is, except for Elly.

She still stood against the wall in the same place she'd stood when the doors first closed. She still clutched her lunch in front of her. She was the only Hawaiian-born person in the elevator and, other than Suzi, was the only one with family and friends on the island outside this room. When the others starting talking of earthquakes, bombings and terrorist attacks, it wasn't personal for them. But she had friends in the restaurant where she worked, less than a hundred yards from Aloha Tower, and two brothers who worked on a fishing charter in the marina nearby. Whatever was happening outside, they could be right in the middle of it. She was horrified at the possibility and worried sick that someone she knew might be killed or injured.

She wasn't worried about herself. She supposed she was quite safe for a while.

The elevator wasn't very far off the ground and didn't seem likely to fall any further.

When the aircraft hit the water, the gasps and grunts in the main cabin as heads hit the seat in front was the only sound. Then shock and disbelief hit.

There had been absolutely no warning.

Shari-Lynn, the chief flight attendant, was sitting in a crew seat facing backwards. As the aircraft rumbled down the runway she closed her eyes and relaxed, enjoying this small respite. She knew she'd be on her feet for the next four hours. She had noticed the change in the engine sound at the end of the runway, but assumed the captain was coaxing a little extra power from the engines for takeoff. As a long-time crew member, she was aware of nuances in sound on the different aircraft. The various clanks, bangs and whines sometimes alarmed the novice flyer and it was her job to reassure them.

When the plane hit the water, she was slammed backwards into her seat. Her eyes flew open and she saw a trail of spray going past the window. Before she had time to react, the aircraft was airborne again. It bounced on and off the water three more times, flinging people in their seats like a bucking bronco, but slowing the aircraft each time.

The professional in Shari-Lynn took over. She swiftly ran over in her mind the water evacuation procedure. It was something they learned in training and reviewed in drills on a regular basis. She knew that each crew member had a specific job and, as most of the crew today had several years' seniority, she could rely on them. There were two new crew on board, but she hoped their training was recent enough that they would remember it.

Thinking about the evacuation problems in ditching in the water, she was unprepared when the aircraft crashed into a solid object head-on. The impact crumpled the nose of the plane and crushed the ceiling of the forward section almost down to the tops of the seats.

She ducked as the ceiling above her came within a few inches of her head. Compartments all through first class popped open and bags and coats spilled on top of people.

That was when she first heard the screaming. Until then everything had been silent except for the loud THWACK and HISS each time the plane hit the water.

Her lifejacket was still in the pocket near her seat where she'd put it after doing the preflight instruction. She unbuckled her seatbelt and tried to stand, remembering too late that there wasn't room. She started to speak to Mit-su, but realized that Mit-su was leaning over the arm of the seat and not moving. Crawling out, she saw that Mit-su was bleeding from a cut on her head. She must have been hit by something from the overhead compartments. Shari-Lynn pulled her upright in her seat and left her there. She had work to do and Mit-su wasn't going to be of any help right now.

People were starting to stir, some moaning and bleeding from injuries sustained from flying objects. Some wild-eyed with fear, but alert.

She was crawling over the bags
scattered in the aisle, intent on getting to the
front cabin door to open it. At the same time,
she called to the passengers in each row to put
on their lifejacket and follow her. A couple of
times she had to stop and show them where
the jackets were kept, under their seats.
*Why didn't they listen to the preflight
demo,* she thought, *then they'd know.*
One woman grabbed her and hung on
tightly. There was terror in her eyes. "Are we
going to drown?" she asked hoarsely. "Is the
plane sinking?"
Shari-Lynn stopped her progress to
reassure her.
"I don't see any water. I think we've run
up on the shore. Now come along and stay
right behind me."
She kept picking her way on hands and
knees along the aisle until the roof was high
enough to stand up, repeating as she went,
"Put on your life jacket. Don't inflate it until I tell
you. Don't bring any personal possessions.
Follow me."
The further back she went the noisier it
was. Some people were moaning with injuries,
others screaming. There was a loud
commotion and screaming coming from the
rear of the plane. The air was thick with dust or
smoke. She hoped it was dust. One of the

dangers of a crash on takeoff was fire from the full fuel tanks.

Just as she thought she wasn't making any progress to the rear of the section and the front cabin door, she became aware of a calm male voice and seconds later heard the distinctive pop of the door opening.

"Oh, thank God, Andy. I forgot about you."

Andy Levitz was another Pac Air pilot who was deadheading home. He'd slipped into the last seat in first class, left vacant by a no-show, just as they were closing the door. Since he was only a few feet from the door, he'd sprung into action as soon as he realized what was happening. He'd gotten Jacquie and the other people in the seats around him to bend forward with their heads in their laps and grasping their ankles, thus sparing them the worst of the wild bucking.

When he got the door open and looked out, he was a little surprised to see the edge of a pier below with people already on it looking up at him. He looked to the right and got the shock of his life.

"Holy cow, we've hit the Aloha Tower."

Just at that moment Shari-Lynn came up behind him.

"Thanks for opening the door Andy. Are we still over water? Or did we make it to shore?" In answer, Andy stepped aside and let her look.

"Wow! Aloha Tower." Her eyes widened at the sight of the famous landmark. Then realizing they had no time for chit-chat, she got down to business and deployed the escape chute.

"I'll handle things at this end," said Andy, mindful that the danger for a flash fire was still there. "You go down the chute first and look after the passengers as they come down." The inflated chute had swung wildly out over the water and it took a minute for the men on the pier to catch the end and hold it down. Shari-Lynn took off her shoes and, holding them in her hands, slid down the chute.

With the men holding the chute, she almost got dumped into the water, so she took a moment to find the ties at the end and tie it securely to a bollard on the pier before signaling to the others to jump.

For a few moments, everyone in the elevator was quiet as they thought about their situation. Almost without thinking, they all chose a wall to stand against. Marianne, a nurse who had taken courses in psychology, wondered if they had instinctively done that because the open space in the middle gave the illusion of more air to breathe. Or because they needed the comfort of a wall at their backs when confronting their fears.

The baby finished his bottle and Kathy put him over her shoulder to burp. Gradually, those closest to the young mother and baby became aware of an aroma, familiar yet unpleasant.

"Christ!" exploded Bubba. "Just what we need in such close quarters, a shitty diaper."

Kathy reddened and turned her back, again looking through the diaper bag hung on the back of the stroller.

Jim glared at Bubba. "And I suppose you were toilet trained at three months and your mother never had to change your diaper?" Bubba made a show of covering his nose and turning his face towards the wall.

Kathy efficiently changed the diaper and then held the dirty one in her hand as she looked around. "I...I'm sorry. I have no place to put this one."

Knisha reached into her handbag and brought out a zip-top sandwich bag filled with mint candies. She dumped the candies into her jacket pocket and passed the bag to Kathy. "Seal it and bury it in the bottom of your diaper bag," she said kindly. "That should take care of it." Then she walked around the tiny space and gave a mint candy to everyone.

"Suck on the candy," she said, "and the mint fumes should fill your nose and cover up any other aroma. By the time it's gone, the other smell should be gone as well."

Bubba, still affronted by Jim's comment to him, refused to take his. Mimi took two, shoved one at him and hissed under her breath, "Eat it and shut up!" He did.

When the aircraft first smacked into the water and Jacquie saw the water rushing by the window, her first thought wasn't "I'm going to die," but "Now Jeremy will never know he was almost a Daddy." She closed her eyes and waited for the worst. Through the noise, she was aware of the man next to her shouting something about 'brace yourself.' Then he pushed her head down on her knees and told her to grab her ankles as tightly as she could. She obeyed without thinking and rode the plane's up and down bucking without any injuries. After the final jarring stop, the man unbuckled her seat belt, found her lifejacket and told her to put it on but not inflate it. Then he did the same for the other passengers around them.

While he was tending to the other passengers, she looked around and saw that the front of the plane was crushed, with the roof right down on the tops of the seats. The crushed roof stopped a few rows in front of her. The aisle was filled with stuff from the overhead compartments and the air was slightly hazy. A flight attendant crawled on her hands and knees down the aisle on top of the debris. When the roof rose high enough, she stood up and staggered the rest of the way. Behind her trailed several passengers.

As Jacquie stood behind her rescuer and watched the door being opened and the emergency chute deployed, she heard a commotion from the rear of the plane. The aisle was on an unbelievable slant. Passengers were staggering up the incline, pulling themselves up by the seat backs. Some were injured, others were panicked and shoving people out of their way.

Then a voice from the rear of the plane screamed and penetrated the other noise.

"Hurry up! There's water coming in."

Then Jacquie thought of Jeremy. He'd had too much to drink and probably fell into a drunken sleep as soon as he sat down. Would he have sense enough to know what was happening and get out? Or was he injured and just sitting there, with the water rising around him.

Frantically, she tried to push her way down the aisle but the tide of panicky humanity pushing the other way was too much. So she started to climb over the backs of the seats. Andy saw her and pulled her back, literally by the seat of the pants.

"What do you think you're doing?" he yelled at her.

"Jeremy, my husband, he's in the very last row, and there's water coming in."

Andy knew the tail was underwater. He had seen it when he looked out and wasn't surprised there was water coming in. But he turned and said to Jacquie, kindly, "He's probably on his way up the aisle right now. If you crawl over the seats you might miss him."

"No! No! You don't understand. He's drunk and probably sound asleep. He might be injured and he doesn't know how to swim." She looked at him with horror in her eyes. "And it's all my fault because I picked a fight with him. And," she wailed, "if he dies he'll never know he was going to be a father."

"You're pregnant and you never told him?"

"No. You see, we had a fight and I didn't realize.....Oh, let me go..." and she wrenched away from him and started climbing the seats again.

Andy turned around and saw two more flight attendants pushing through the crowds in the aisles. He yelled to them to take over at the door and he followed Jacquie to the back of the plane over the backs of the seats.

He caught up to her about halfway along. She was panting with exertion and fright. He had to admit he didn't feel too good himself. He still wasn't sure the aircraft wasn't going to blow and the thought of being trapped in the tail with a fire and no way out gave him the chills. That thought rolled over him just as climbed over the seat with the emergency exit. He stopped, studied the exit for a few seconds and then grasped the two handles and ripped it open. He turned the exit window sideways and threw it out the hole. Now he had his escape if he needed it. Then he followed Jacquie to the murky rear of the aircraft.

They were far enough down now that there was no one left in the aisles, only debris from the popped overheads. He switched from the seats to the aisle and made better time. Jacquie had made it to the rear before him and he heard her scream. He ran the rest of the way.

What he saw in the rear of the plane was a nightmare. Water had filled the rear galley and bathrooms and was lapping at the back row of seats. There were two bodies floating in the water and Andy knew without touching them that it was too late for them.

There was a man, still buckled in his seatbelt and in water to his waist. He was unconscious, his head was cut and his ear almost torn off, and he was bleeding profusely. Jacquie was trying to keep her balance on the wet carpet and, at the same time, trying to undo his seatbelt.

This must be the elusive Jeremy, soon to be a daddy, who had too much to drink and who was in the doghouse for some reason. At least he was still alive. Dead men don't bleed like that.

He took off his tie and knotted it around Jeremy's head, carefully positioning it to put pressure on the bleeding ear. Then he unsnapped the seatbelt.

With Andy clasping him underneath the arms and Jacquie carrying his legs, they managed to get him back up the long aisle. All the passengers who could leave on their own were gone and firefighters and paramedics were preparing to enter the aircraft to carry out the injured. Andy hailed them from the door and placed Jeremy in the chute. He was neatly caught at the bottom and popped onto a stretcher. Jacquie went next with Andy right behind her.

Only when they were outside could they see the full extent of the damage.

The nose of the aircraft was buried in Aloha Tower about 30 feet above the pier, knocking out part of the wall and crushing the roof of the aircraft to well past the cockpit. The tail was in the water up past the back windows.

Andy looked at the nose of the craft with sadness. He could tell by its condition that it was unlikely the two pilots had survived.

He turned to speak to Jacquie but she was already climbing into the ambulance with her husband.

Chapter 3

Over the next hour, everyone except the Chens took a turn yelling for help. At first, only the men did the yelling. Then Knisha voiced the opinion that as women's voices were higher, maybe they would penetrate the steel and concrete walls where the men's wouldn't.

So for a while the small steel box reverberated with alternating male and female voices, interspersed with banging on the walls and door with the metal pipe from the stroller. Even the two teens took a turn.

There was no response.

The baby had gone back to sleep after his bottle and diaper change, but the adults were becoming restless. First one, and then another, moved away from the wall and paced around the confined space. They started talking to one another, exchanging names and home towns. Eventually C.J. and Suzi found themselves side by side and started talking.

C.J. was fascinated by the diminutive Chinese girl with the round face that always seemed to be smiling, and who spoke two languages. He started asking her about China and was surprised to learn that she had grown up in Honolulu and gone to an American school. Her parents had emigrated from Hong Kong when she was a baby and she had no memory of her former home.

"Do your grandparents live here too?" he asked.

"No. They still live in Hong Kong. This is their first time in Hawaii. They just celebrated their 50th anniversary and my father brought them over here for a visit to honor them and their long life."

C.J. noticed that she pronounced Hawaii like a native, "Havaii" with a V in the middle.

"How come your parents aren't here today?"

"My parents both work. I've been taking my grandparents around the city sightseeing." She grinned ruefully. "I guess I picked the wrong day to come to Aloha Tower."

They were still talking quietly when Mrs. Chen made a slight sound and they looked over to see her knees buckling as she slid to the floor. Her husband squatted down beside her and Suzi was there in an instant as well.

The three conversed in Chinese for a couple of minutes.

Suzi stood up and faced the others, who were watching anxiously

"She's all right," she explained hesitantly. "But she has a heart condition and she just decided she can't stand up any longer." She hesitated again as she looked around shyly at the others. "Does anyone have anything to drink. She's a little thirsty and she has to take a pill."

Elly, who was still standing in a corner and hadn't spoken to anyone, stepped forward and held out her lunch bag.

"I have a bottle of water in here if it'll help." She took it out and passed it to Suzi who smiled her thanks and went to tend to her grandmother.

Bubba, who had been leaning back with his arms folded and his eyes closed, not participating in any conversation, suddenly stood up straight and looked at Elly with interest.

"What else you got in that lunch bag, girlie? Any snacks?"

Mimi elbowed him in the ribs. "Of all the people in this room, you're the one who doesn't need any snacks." She retorted.

Elly looked at Mimi a bit nervously and said to Bubba, "I've got some sushi and an apple. You're welcome to them if you want."

"Yuck!" Bubba snorted in disgust. "I've had some great meals here in Hawaii. Some of them real different, too. Not what I'm used to back home in Arkansas, of course, but good anyway. But I got no use for that raw fish stuff. I can't go that a'tall."

Like most boys his age, C.J. was always hungry. At the mention of food his stomach growled, loud enough to be heard by everyone. Several of them broke out laughing. It was the first time anyone had laughed since the elevator doors shut and it eased the tensions a little. C.J. laughed too and took a bow, embarrassed to be the center of attention but pleased that he'd caused a positive reaction.

When Suzi finished with her grandmother, she returned the half-empty bottle to Elly and came back to stand by C.J. They started talking again in low tones while the adult conversations swirled around them. Suzi wanted to know why C.J. had initials instead of a name.

"That's 'cause my name is Cato, like my Dad. Cato Junior. So they call me C.J. so it won't be confusing. I know some kids in school who are also called after their fathers and grandfathers, sometimes for several generations. I have one friend who has The Fourth after his name. We call him Four by Four. But only when his mother isn't listening. She's one tough lady." He laughed. Suzi laughed with him and went on to tell him about some of her friends who had two names, a Chinese name for home and an American name for the rest of the world.

Cato, who hadn't contributed much other than taking his turn yelling for help, glanced idly around the group. His eyes stopped on C.J. and Suzi, their heads together laughing. Afterwards he would wonder if it was the race thing, his anger at Bubba for calling him "boy" and his disdain for rednecks like him and what he stood for in the south, or just the fact that his son was too young to be showing interest in a girl. Whatever it was, it was fueled by the tensions of being cooped up in the small space for over two hours.

"What do you think you're doing?" he roared, curling his fingers around C.J's upper arm and jerking him away from Suzi. C.J. was mortified.

"I'm not doing anything, Dad. We were just talking." He looked at his arm where his father still gripped him. "Please, you're hurting me."

Cato was about to say something else when Bubba chuckled.

"Leave the boy alone. At least she ain't white."

Cato's eyes grew round in shock and he launched himself at Bubba. Not even Knisha was going to stop him this time. Bubba was unprepared for the attack and took a few blows before he began defending himself. Cato had a wiry athletic strength and should have had the upper hand, but Bubba outweighed him, had been in a few barroom brawls himself and knew how to fight dirty. Cato hit the floor with a howl, clutching his crotch. Bubba would have leaped on top of him, but Mimi grabbed him by the belt and the other two men, Jim and Dave, once they got over their shocked surprise at the attack, waded in and helped hold him back.

Cato picked himself up and looked ready to start again, but Knisha put her arm around her husband and led him to the opposite side of the elevator from Bubba. Wedging herself into a corner, she put both arms around Cato and kept his back to the room, and not incidentally to Bubba who still glowered at him. The others could hear Knisha talking to her husband softly and he finally relaxed.

C.J. came over and joined the family group. "I'm sorry, Dad." He wasn't sure what he was sorry for, but it looked as if he were the cause, so it seemed the thing to do. Knisha smiled sadly at her son and hugged him.

Suzi and C.J. avoided looking at each other.

Dave, the mechanical engineer, had been studying the elevator control panel. He borrowed Bubba's screwdriver again and proceeded to take the panel apart. When he had the cover off, he poked around inside, flipping switches, unscrewing things and pulled out two bare wires. Holding them at arm's length with just his fingertips, he cautiously brought the two bare ends together.

Nothing happened.

"Dead as a doornail." he announced. "The main power supply's been cut. We aren't going anywhere until someone forces that door."

It was a depressing thought to everyone inside the small steel enclosure. After almost three hours it seemed to be getting smaller by the minute.

To cheer them up Knisha passed around another handful of her mint candies.

Everyone took one.

After putting the control panel back together, Dave started inspecting the ceiling. It was made of one-foot-square mirror tiles that reflected everyone in the elevator eerily. It also reflected what little light they had, which helped. But Dave had another thought. Older elevators, he knew, had an escape hatch in the roof. He wasn't sure about the newer ones. However, Aloha Tower had been around a long time, and it was possible that this was an old elevator that had simply been refurbished. He wondered if there was an escape hatch behind those tiles.

He picked up the piece of pipe that had been used to tap on the doors, reached up and used it to reposition one of the emergency lights, shining it on the ceiling. It had the effect of almost doubling the available light. A couple of the others smiled and thanked him, thinking that had been his intention. He grunted his acknowledgment and went on inspecting the ceiling for any irregularities.

He finally found what he was looking for – one of the mirror tiles had a slightly different cant to it. It was tilted slightly to one side. Not enough to notice at a glance, or even two or three. But with the spotlight shining across it, there was a tiny break in the shadows. Once he found it, it was easy to see, even without the spotlight.

Dave stepped into the center of the room and cleared his throat.

"It's possible we can do something to help ourselves. It doesn't look as if we're going to get much help from outside." He grinned ruefully. The others came alert instantly, everyone asking at once what he had in mind.

He held up his hand for silence and carefully explained what he'd been thinking. About older elevators having an escape hatch in the roof and the fact that this was probably an old elevator that had been refurbished. He pointed out the mirror tile in the ceiling that was slightly askew, and after looking at it from different angles, eventually everyone could see it.

"It's possible," he went on, "that there is an escape hatch behind those tiles. And if there is, I'm betting that some part of it, perhaps the latch, is behind that crooked tile."

"Well, what are we waiting for?" asked Bubba, in a voice just slightly below his usual bellow.

"First we need a plan," answered Dave. "We have a few problems and we may need some tools. The first problem is the height of the ceiling. No one here can reach it and we have no step-stool. I only reached the spotlight with the help of the piece of pipe. Then we need something strong enough to pry off that tile. To keep it on the ceiling through all the movement this elevator goes through, it must be pretty strong adhesive."

"And what if it breaks," put in Jim nervously, looking at his baby. "There'll be broken glass flying all over."

"We need a piece of cloth, the biggest piece we have, to hold underneath it to catch the broken bits." He looked at Elly, who was wearing a floor-length Hawaiian dress, calculating how much fabric was in it. Elly stepped back behind Mimi and shook her head. Mimi patted Elly on the shoulder and picked up her tote bag that had been lying on the floor.

"I have somethin' more practical than Elly's dress. I went shoppin' this mornin' and bought me a big ol' beach towel for a souvenir." She produced a large towel with a garish black and orange sunset on it.

Everyone agreed it was perfect.

Bubba cleared throat. "We ain't got no step-stool, but you," he pointed at Jim, "you don't look like you weigh more'n a fly. I can prob'ly hold you around the knees and lift you up that high." No one doubted he could, but Jim had a better idea.

"Why don't we use the baby's stroller. It's a good sturdy one and it has a brake on the wheels." That problem solved, the next one was the matter of a tool to pry off the mirror.

"I've got a nail file," offered Marianne, with a grin at her husband. He grinned back, remembering her "fixing" jobs over the years. She always said that with a nail file and a roll of duct tape she could fix anything. It went against his methodical engineer's mind-set, but it was amazing how often she actually could.

"We could try it, but I don't think it's strong enough to go the distance. Any more ideas?"

Knisha also had a nail file and so did Kathy. Someone suggested taping two together to make them stronger.

They had almost run out of ideas when C.J. reluctantly put his hand in his pocket and brought out his treasured Swiss Army knife. He knew that prying off the tiles would break one or more blades and he hated to lose his knife, but he also didn't want to stay in this elevator any longer than necessary.

Dave's eyes lit up as he hefted the knife. "Perfect," he told C.J. "This should do the job."

He positioned the baby stroller underneath the crooked tile, set the brake, and carefully placing his feet on the frame instead of the vinyl seat, stood up on it. Despite the brakes, the wheels moved slightly and Dave swung wildly, losing his balance. He would have crashed to the floor, but Cato, stepping swiftly forward grabbed him and broke his fall. Both men fell against the wall and slid slowly to the floor.

Dave stood up first, grasped Cato's hand and helped him up. "Thanks, man. You probably saved me from a broken bone."

Cato looked at the stroller and said, "Obviously that's not going to work very well. But if four of us each block a wheel with our feet, it should steady it." Immediately, four pairs of feet were each blocking a wheel. One of them was Knisha who was wearing sandals.

"I'll probably lose a toe," she grumbled good-naturedly. "But what's a toe or two against spending the rest of my life in here?"

Two others held Mimi's towel under the tile and Dave started prying at the corner. The first corner of the tile came off neatly, but the rest was harder going. It soon became apparent that the towel wasn't catching all the flying glass. Dave stopped for a minute and got down from the stroller.

"I suggest that everyone put on a hat if they have it, or cover your head somehow. Also, if you don't wear glasses, put on your sunglasses or borrow a pair. We've got no way to treat injuries here." Everyone found something to put on. The Chens were still sitting the floor, but Mr. Chen had taken off his jacket and draped it over his wife's head. He pulled his own hat down over his eyes and put an arm around his wife.

Cato, who wore glasses, pulled out his baseball cap and put it on. "Here let me do that for a while," he said to Dave. "I'm taller than you and stretching that high is not such a strain for me." Dave gratefully passed over the knife. Cato climbed on the stroller and started chipping.

With half the tile gone, a seam in the ceiling was emerging. Cato pushed on it tentatively and it moved. He grinned at Dave.

"Good work there. We may have our escape hatch." Instead of chipping at the same tile, he now started chipping along the seam line. Once he struck the mirror hard with the butt of the knife and the tile cracked through the middle. He was able to work off half that tile in one piece.

When Cato tired, Jim took over. It was a long stretch for him, but they were almost there.

Finally they had a square plate exposed. It was not very big, barely a foot square, but it had taken four glass tiles to uncover it.

They were all standing there looking at the metal plate in the ceiling when Suzi let out a cry of anguish. She was kneeling on the floor next to her grandparents.

"My grandmother," she said between sobs. "I think she's dead."

Marianne rushed over to her. "I'm a nurse. Let me see." She checked for a pulse, peeled back an eyelid and put her ear to the thin chest. She looked at Suzi and her grandfather sorrowfully. "I'm sorry. I think you're right. She's gone."

With one arm still around his wife, Mr. Chen spoke to his granddaughter in Chinese, gesturing to the others around and to the ceiling.

"He says she's been gone for a while. But he said there was nothing we could do and we were all busy trying to find a way out, so he just sat there and held her."

While they were all standing there wondering what to do, Bubba, in his own inimitable way, cut to the heart of the matter.

"I know we all feel sorry for the old lady, but we're not helpin' anythin' by standing here with our thumbs up our asses, so why don't we do somethin' about that there plate."

Dave winced at Bubba's choice of words, but said only, "Can I borrow your screwdriver again. Those look like countersunk screws in the corners."

Within minutes the screws were loosened and the plate removed. Excitement soon turned to dismay. What they had was a hole that only about three people in the elevator, not including the baby, could fit through.

Jim snorted. "Now's the time for Bubba's strength. If you could life me up, old man, I could stick my head through. But I don't think the rest of me could fit."

"No!" said C.J. "Let me. If Dad can lift me up, I can see what's up there and I think I can fit through. Then if there's a way out I can go for help." He looked at his father. "Please Dad, I really want to do this."

Cato nodded. To the others he said, "I think he can do this. He's a good boy and he's a good athlete. If there's any climbing or lifting to do or squeezing through small spaces, he can probably do better than any of us."

C.J. preened at this unexpected praise from his father. He stood under the hole looking up but could see nothing.

Cato squatted down and told his son to climb on his shoulders like he used to when he was younger. When he stood up, C.J.'s head was just within the hole. C.J. put his arms up in the hole and took some of his weight on his elbows to spare his father.

"It's dark up here, I can't see much."

"Maybe my phone will be of some use after all," joked Dave. "It has a flashlight app on it that doesn't need to be on line to work." He turned the phone on, activated the flashlight and passed it up to C.J.

"What's up there, son? What do you see?"

"I see wheels, big wheels." His voice echoed strangely outside the chamber.

Some inside remarked that this must be a really old elevator if they were still using wheels and cables.

All of a sudden, C.J. dropped back inside, nearly collapsing his father. His eyes were round with astonishment.

"Those are AIRPLANE wheels! There's an airplane up there!"

"So that explains it," said Jim. "Probably one of the small sightseeing planes crashed into the tower." He looked up sharply, trying to see into the hole. "Or is it a military aircraft? Can you tell the difference?"

"Yes, I can tell the difference," said C.J. scornfully. "And it isn't a small plane or a military plane. It's a big one like the kind we flew over here on. All I can see is the nose and the nose wheel, but I had a good look at the ones on the runway when we got here, and this one looks like a big passenger plane.

They were all stunned by this information and just stood there looking at one another. They were beginning to realize just how lucky they really were. A few seconds later and 10 feet higher in the shaft and none of them would have survived.

"I'm sure you're right, C.J." said Jim, "but aircraft are my job and I'd like to get a look at this." He looked around at the others. "Do you think a couple of you can lift me up?"

Cato slid C.J. to the floor while Dave and Bubba each grabbed one of Jim's legs and hoisted him until his head was in the hole.

He whistled and ducked back in. When he was on the floor again he said, "C.J. knows his stuff. That's a passenger plane all right. Looks like a long-range Airbus to me. He must have been taking off from Honolulu International and didn't bank soon enough."

"And if there were a lot of casualties," put in Marianne," it would be straining their rescue capabilities. That's why they haven't come looking for us."

C.J. pulled on his father's sleeve. "Dad, hoist me up again, will you and I'll go all the way up this time. Maybe I can find a way out." But now that he knew what was up there, Cato was reluctant to put his son in any danger.

"How do we know it's stable? What if a wall gives way? Maybe they'll get to us soon anyway."

"If they don't know we're here now," said Dave quietly, "it could be hours more before they come looking for us. It's been over four hours now and that plane up there hasn't shifted since it crashed. I doubt if it will now. I vote to let the boy try."

Cato looked at Knisha and she nodded. "OK son, we'll give it another try." Before he squatted down again he looked his son in the eye and said, "Be careful. And no heroics. OK?" C.J. nodded solemnly.

This time C.J. hoisted himself up through the hatch and sat on the edge for a while until his eyes became accustomed to the dim light. He looked around and described to the others what he saw.

"There are no doors in this elevator shaft. There must be only the one at the bottom and the one at the top. I can't see the one at the top. The plane is in the way. There's only a small window right above me, but it's a long way up, higher than the nose of the plane."

"C.J." called Dave, "can you see a metal ladder set into the wall anywhere? Some old elevator shafts have them from the second floor up."

"Yes, I can see a ladder. It's way above my head, but I can reach it if I stand on the plane's wheel. And there's some sort of ledge under the window that I can crawl along." Knisha blanched when she heard what her son intended to do and started to protest, but he lifted his legs up through the hatch and stood up, out of reach.

This was the most important and most exciting thing that C.J. had ever done in his life, and no one was going to stop him. He was going to climb through that window and find the rescue people who could open the elevator door.

He walked around the nose wheel trying to figure out how to climb it. It was taller than him. The rubber part was no problem, but when he put his foot on the shiny rim it slipped off and he landed back on the elevator roof with a thud.

"What was that, C.J." called his father. "Are you all right?"

"I'm OK Dad," a hollow disembodied voice came down from the hatch. "I'm just having trouble climbing the wheel."

Suddenly Elly, who hadn't contributed much to any of the discussions, came forward. "Sir," she said to Cato, "I'm small enough to fit through that hatch. Why don't I sit on the edge and I can relay information back and forth."

Cato looked her up and down. "In that dress?"

Elly laughed and asked Mimi for the scarf that was tied around her hat. She tied the scarf around her waist, reached between her legs and pulled the back hem of her dress up and tucked it into the scarf, knotting it securely. What she was now wearing was a pair of baggy shorts.

"We used to do this when we were kids and wanted to go wading." she said.

A couple of minutes later she was comfortably perched on the edge of the hatch talking to C.J. Seeing his problem with the wheel, she pulled herself up on the elevator roof. The next time he tried to climb the wheel, she gave him a boost, then pressed her shoulder tight against the rubber to give him a place to rest his knee as he pulled himself the rest of the way up. Triumphantly, he gave her a thumbs-up. Elly sat back down on the edge of the hatch and told the others that C.J. was now up on the wheel.

She then related his progress as he climbed the ladder. As he inched his way along the narrow ledge, holding to the steel girders, she said nothing – not wanting to upset his mother with this dangerous part of the climb.

When he reached the window, she announced that he was there. There was a collective sigh of relief below.

C.J. was now at the window looking out. He called down to her.

"There are people running around out there, but there not paying any attention to me. It's almost as if they can't see me."

"Do you have anything to bang on the window with, or to break it?"

"No, I don't. Dave still has my knife."

"Use your fist. Or use your shoe. But whatever you do," she cautioned, "don't lose your grip. It's a long way down."

C.J. pounded on the window with his fist, to no avail. He couldn't reach his shoe without losing his balance.

Elly related the problem to the others.

"How high is he?" asked Cato.

"He's standing a ledge about 20 feet above me."

Cato closed his eyes and thought for a minute. "Can you throw? I mean, have you ever played ball?"

"Sir, " she said. "I'll have you know I'm on my high school's softball team."

"Good," said Cato, smiling. "Because now you're going to prove how good a pitcher you are."

He turned to the others. "Does anyone have any string? Elly is going to throw C.J.'s knife up to him and I want it tied to a string in case he doesn't catch it on the first try."

Everyone started rummaging in tote bags and pockets, but no one could find any string. Knisha started unraveling the end of a silk scarf, but got less than a yard before it broke.

Meanwhile Mr. Chen, still sitting on the floor holding his wife, was following the action. He thought he understood what they wanted. Beckoning to his granddaughter, he passed her his wife's handbag. Suzi looked inside and her eyes filled with tears. She pulled out a tiny baby sock and a ball of yarn with a second sock started. Her grandmother had knit several of these as they traveled around the city all week. They were for her newest grandchild. The old man gestured and said something.

"He says she'll never finish the sock so do something useful with the yarn."

Cato solemnly accepted the yarn and measured off about 30 feet. He tied one end to the knife and made a loop in the other.

Passing it up to Elly, he said, "Hold the loop tightly when you throw it, in case he doesn't catch it. You'll be able to retrieve it and throw it again."

Elly disappeared inside the hatch and they heard the knife clang against the wall. That meant C.J. hadn't caught it. A moment later they heard a cheer from both of them and Elly's head appeared in the hole.

"He caught it!"

In fact C.J. had to reach so far to catch it that he almost lost his balance. But catch it he did, and he was still hanging on. Elly prudently didn't pass on that information.

Using the butt of the knife, C.J. starting banging on the window and soon attracted someone's attention.

A man in a security guard's uniform came over to the window and peered in. At first he didn't see C.J. but when C.J. put his face right against the window he finally saw him. "What are you doing in there, kid? Get the hell out of there." And he turned and walked away.

C.J. slumped in discouragement. To go through all this and be ignored was too much. So he began pounding on the window again with the knife and yelling. This time he cracked the window and attracted the attention of a firefighter. The firefighter, when he realized there was a child in the elevator shaft, called to someone else and the two of them peered in. C.J. frantically pointed downward and yelled "Help!" The two finally got the message that there was trouble.

They brought a fire ax and yelled to C.J. "Stand back, kid."

C.J. scurried back along the ledge and shouted to Elly to watch out. She moved behind the nose wheel, out of range of flying glass. Within minutes, the firefighters had the window smashed and were leaning into the shaft. They looked in disbelief at C.J and Elly and the elevator below.

The men pulled C.J. out through the window and called to Elly to tell the others to hang on for a few more minutes. They'd find someone to open the door.

In truth, it was another half hour before the doors were finally forced open. But the occupants didn't mind. They could hear what was going on. Someone at least knew they were there.

As they filed out they were met by a barrage of media.

TV and news reporters had been on the scene all day. They'd interviewed survivors from the plane, including Jeremy and Jacquie. The world knew about Jacquie's baby before Jeremy did. They interviewed Shari-Lynn and also Andy, who was being hailed as a hero. They interviewed people who'd been in the Aloha Shopping Center. They got eye-witness accounts from people who had been on the observation deck at the top of the tower and saw the plane coming towards them, helpless to get away. They'd come down the stairs, seldom used in recent years, but still there. They talked to people on the boats in the marina and people at the airport. They got the whole story....almost.

But the reporters missed the fact that three of the stranded occupants stayed behind in the elevator waiting for an ambulance. They didn't notice the teen-age boy standing with a firefighter waiting for the doors of the elevator to be opened.

When the elevator survivors came out they ran right past the assembled reporters and cameras, heading for the restaurant across the courtyard where Elly worked. The media followed on their heels.

The last one in line, Bubba, turned and yelled, "We'll talk to you after we've been to the pisser." The reporters laughed and slowed down, waiting outside the restaurant. They could understand their hurry, after being trapped for over five hours.

They had completely missed this one.

After their necessary stop, Elly led them through the restaurant and out the back door.

Two days later they met again in the Chinese cemetery west of Pearl Harbor to say goodbye to Mrs. Chen.

There were no flowers on the coffin, just a single baby sock and a tangled ball of yarn.

The media missed this one too.

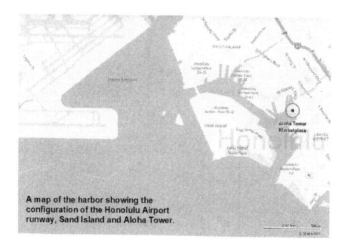

A map of the harbor showing the
configuration of the Honolulu Airport
runway, Sand Island and Aloha Tower.

Helen Kaulbach is a retired newspaper reporter and travel writer. She lives with her husband Doug in British Columbia, Canada, and they travel often to Hawaii.

Made in the USA
Middletown, DE
13 March 2019